Silas' Seven Grandparents

story by Anita Horrocks

illustrations by Helen Flook

ORCA BOOK PUBLISHERS

Library and Archives Canada Cataloguing in Publication

Horrocks, Anita, 1958-
Silas' seven grandparents / written by Anita Horrocks ; illustrated by Helen Flook.

ISBN 978-1-55143-561-9

I. Flook, Helen II. Title.

PS8565.O686S45 2010   JC813'.54   C2009-906728-5

First published in the United States, 2010
Library of Congress Control Number: 2009940412

Summary: Silas is a small boy who finds a unique solution to keeping up with his seven adoring grandparents and stepgrandparents.

Orca Book Publishers is dedicated to preserving the environment and has printed this book on paper certified by the Forest Stewardship Council.

Orca Book Publishers gratefully acknowledges the support for its publishing programs provided by the following agencies: the Government of Canada through the Canada Book Fund and the Canada Council for the Arts, and the Province of British Columbia through the BC Arts Council and the Book Publishing Tax Credit.

Interior and cover artwork created using acrylic water-based inks
Design by Teresa Bubela

ORCA BOOK PUBLISHERS
PO Box 5626, Stn. B
Victoria, BC Canada
V8R 6S4

ORCA BOOK PUBLISHERS
PO Box 468
Custer, WA USA
98240-0468

www.orcabook.com
Printed and bound in Canada.

13 12 11 10 • 5 4 3 2

For Sydney and Wren,
and all their seven grandparents.
—AH

For Eileen, Macsen's grandmother.
—HF

Most of the time, Silas liked having seven grandparents. Most of the time, having seven grandparents made Silas feel especially loved, times seven.

← me and Nana

Gramma, Papa and me →

me and
Opa and Oma

me and
Granny and
Grandad

Silas' seven grandparents gave him presents on his birthday. Six grandparents baked birthday cakes, and one bought an ice-cream cake.

But sometimes Silas couldn't eat all his cake.
"After all, I only have one stomach!" said Silas.

Silas' seven grandparents came to his hockey games. Five grandparents cheered and two coached his team.

But sometimes seven grandparents couldn't fit in the dressing room.

"After all, I only have one pair of skates to lace!" said Silas.

Silas' seven grandparents helped take care of Silas when he was sick. One rubbed his back, two fed him chicken soup and four sang softly to him.

But sometimes seven grandparents traipsing in and out made too much commotion.

"After all, I only want to sleep!" said Silas.

Silas' seven grandparents took him on outings over the July long weekend. Two took him camping. Two took him to the dog show. Two took him to the dinosaur museum. And one rode the roller coaster with him at the amusement park.

But sometimes Silas couldn't keep up with his seven grandparents.

"After all, I'm only one small boy," said Silas.

And when Silas' mom and dad decided to go away for a few days on a business trip, seven grandparents invited Silas to stay with them.

"Come stay with me, Silas," said Nana. Silas' nana was a scientist. She lived in a loft in the city. Her ceiling looked like the night sky. "We'll go to the planetarium and sleep on the roof. I need you to help me count shooting stars."

Every night at bedtime, Silas made a wish on the star Nana had hung above his bed especially for him.

"Come stay with us," said Oma and Opa. Silas' oma and opa grew all kinds of good things to eat in their market garden. "The saskatoons, raspberries and strawberries are ripe. We need you to help bake bumbleberry pies and build a doghouse for Laddie's five new puppies."

Every night at bedtime, Silas filled the bird feeder outside his window, the one Opa had made especially so the birds would visit him in the morning. Then he snuggled into his quilt, the one Oma had made especially to keep him warm.

"Come stay with us," said Gramma and Papa.
Silas' gramma and papa lived by a golf course. "You can
swim in the pool and play golf with us. We need you to
drive the golf cart."

Every night at bedtime, Silas' father read him a
story from the book Gramma and Papa had sent him,
the one they chose especially to give him sweet dreams
about far-off adventures.

"Come stay with us," said Granny and Grandad.
Silas' granny and grandad lived by a lake in the foothills.
"We'll take you to a powwow and go fishing and canoeing.
We need you to help us paddle."

Every night at bedtime, Silas twirled the dream catcher Granny and Grandad had given him, the one especially made to keep bad dreams away.

"I can't stay with all seven grandparents at the same time!" said Silas.

"You'll have to choose," his mother said. "Your grandparents know you can't be everywhere at once. After all, there's only one Silas."

That night, Silas couldn't sleep. He was still awake when the moon drifted by his window. The man-in-the-moon peeked into Silas' room.

Moonbeams played hide-and-seek in his bird feeder. Moonbeams streamed across his storybook and danced in and out of his dream catcher. Moonbeams twinkled off his star, so that glimmers of light tumbled all over his quilt.

And wrapped in a glittering hug from his head to his toes, Silas felt especially loved, times seven.

Silas laughed. "Thank you," he said to the man-in-the-moon. "You've given me an especially good idea."

The next morning, Silas colored and painted. He cut,
he glued and he glittered. He printed and folded and stamped.

Then he mailed his especially good idea to his seven grandparents.

On the day his parents left on their business trip,
Silas waited on his front porch. Soon Oma and Opa's truck
chugged up to the house.

"Hello, Silas!" called Oma and Opa.

Behind them, Granny and Grandad's camper swung into
the driveway. "Hey, partner!" called Granny and Grandad.

Gramma and Papa beeped their car horn as they parked
out front. "Hi, Silas!" called Gramma and Papa.

Finally, Nana rode up on her bicycle. "Hola, Silas!"
called Nana with a grin.

Silas' parents ran outside to see what all the hubbub was about. "What on earth?!" they said.

"I can't stay with all seven grandparents at the same time," said Silas, "but all seven grandparents can stay with me!"

So they did. Seven grandparents took care of Silas while his parents were away.

On the first day, seven grandparents baked bumbleberry pies and built a doghouse mansion with Silas.

On the second day, seven grandparents swam in the pool and rode golf carts with Silas.

On the third day, seven grandparents danced at a powwow, fished and paddled canoes with Silas.

And on the last day, seven grandparents went to the planetarium and stayed up late to count shooting stars with Silas.

But sometimes seven grandparents weren't enough to keep up with one Silas.

"After all," whispered Silas as he tucked them in,
"I'm especially loved, times seven."